First Edition

Printed and bound in Cornwall by R. Booth Ltd (01326) 373226

Story and characters devised
by Jools Hichens

Illustrated by Graham Hichens

Everybody in Pasty Cottage, near the seaside town of Hayle in Cornwall, had woken up extra early, and they were all looking forward to a spectacular fun filled day.

Pixie Pasty had made her bed, tied her pink bows in her crust and was skipping down the stairs when Penrose Pasty whizzed by her.

"Hooray! Hooray!" He cried. "At long, long last! I have been waiting for ages and ages and ages for today to be here and I don't want to miss one single bit of it!"

Grandpop Pasty looked quite puzzled.
"Miss one bit of what?" He asked
buttering some toast.

"We don't want to miss going to
RNAS Culdrose Air Day!"
Cried Pixie and Penrose. "It's a
spectacular show and we missed it last
year because Peter Patty did a
very, very dangerous thing!"

“Did he?” Said Grandpop Pasty. “And, what very dangerous thing did he do?”

Penrose gasped. “Don’t you know what happened Grandpop?” He asked.

“No,” said Grandpop taking a sip of his tea. “I don’t think I do.”

And with that Grandpop Pasty was told what happened on that dreadful day. And it went like this.........

It was early morning when Peter Patty stood in the doorway of Pasty Cottage.

He was holding a brand new bright yellow kite with lots and lots of coloured bows on the tail.

Peter was very, very proud of his new kite, because he had saved up all his pocket money to buy it.

"Good morning everyone." He said.
"I'm going to fly my new
yellow kite
in the
field on
the cliff
top.
I
thought
Pixie and
Penrose
might
like to
come
with me,
it will be
such good
fun."

"Ooh! Yes please!"
Said Pixie and Penrose hopefully.

“Off you go then!” Said Daddy Pasty.
“And remember, you must
stay away from the edge of the
cliff top, you are to play in the
field where it is safe.
Please do not go anywhere
near the edge of the cliff.”

“Okay!” They cried, and
headed for the door.

“Don’t forget to be back here
for 9 ‘o’ clock.” Said Mummy Pasty.
“We don’t want to be late
for RNAS Culdrose Air Day.”

Mummy and Daddy Pasty watched as
Pixie, Penrose and Peter walked
down the garden path and up
the lane to the fields,
trailing the new
yellow kite behind them.

It was quite breezy in the field on the top of the cliff.

Peter Patty unravelled the long kite steering strings and held onto them tightly while Penrose picked up the kite, ran with it, and then threw the kite into the air for the wind to take it.

The kite took off with a whoosh! It whizzed and swooped and swirled across the clear blue sky.

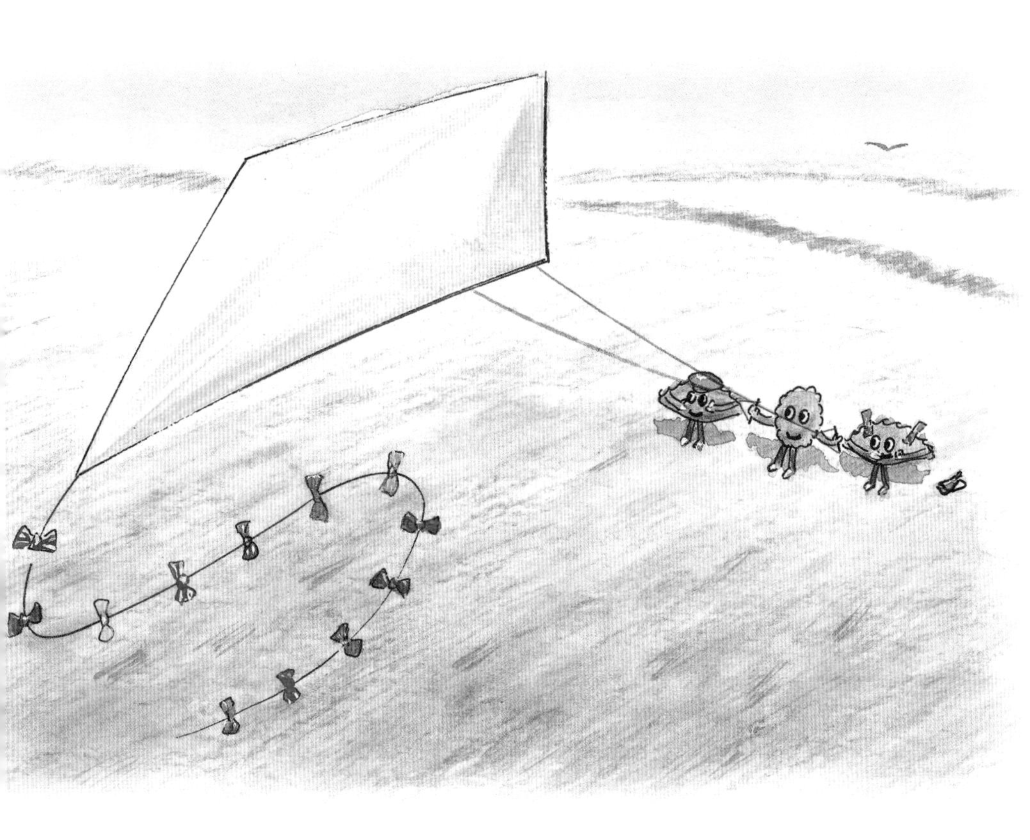

“Oh look!” Said Pixie. “The kite is dancing in the wind. I wish I could be a kite with a tail of lovely bows!”

"You can!" Said Penrose. "I have just the things!"

And with that Penrose searched through his brown bag and pulled out a ball of string and some coloured paper hankies.

"Here you are Pixie." He said. "You can make a tail from these and pretend to be a kite!"

And that is just what Pixie did.

Meanwhile, Peter held the kite strings tightly as he steered the kite this way and that way, and up and down.

"It's terrific!" Said Penrose, watching the kite somersault through the air.

After sometime Peter gently brought the kite back down to land.

“It’s your turn Penrose!” Shouted Peter.

“Oh great!” Said Penrose. He laid his favourite brown bag on the grass and took hold of the long kite strings.

Peter ran and threw the kite into the air. Once again the wind took it high into the sky with a whoosh!

The kite swirled in the air with the tail of bows behind, diving down and swooping up. It was a wonderful colourful sight.

Suddenly Penrose felt the kite pull hard on the strings! He could feel the strings tugging, and tugging trying to pull away!

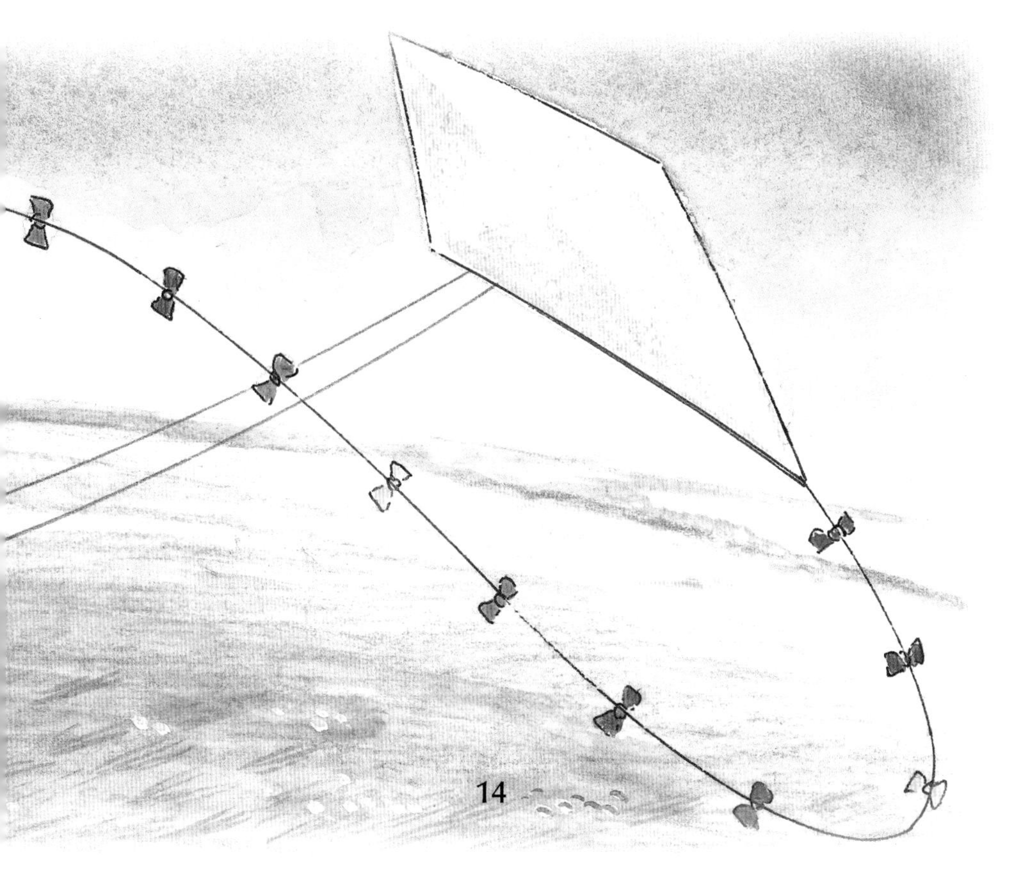

"Peter! Peter!" He shouted. "I'm going to bring the kite back down to land, I think the wind has become a bit too blustery!"

"Okay!" Cried Peter.

Penrose brought the kite down with a bump. "Oops!" He said. "I hope it's not broken!"

It wasn't.

Peter started to wind in the kite strings and was just about to pick the kite up when a gust of wind suddenly lifted the kite back into the air!
Peter felt the strings disappear through his fingers.

"Oh no!" Cried Pixie. "It's flying away from us!"

"Quickly!" Cried Peter. "Quickly!
Let's try to catch it by the tail!"

Peter, Pixie and Penrose
chased after the kite.

They ran through the field
jumping up into the air trying to
grab at the tail as the kite swirled and
swooped above them by itself,
but they could not catch it.

They climbed onto the
hedge, but the kite was still
out of their reach.

Then, as suddenly as the kite had
taken off into the air, it fell
out of the sky, and
crashed
over the edge of the
cliff!

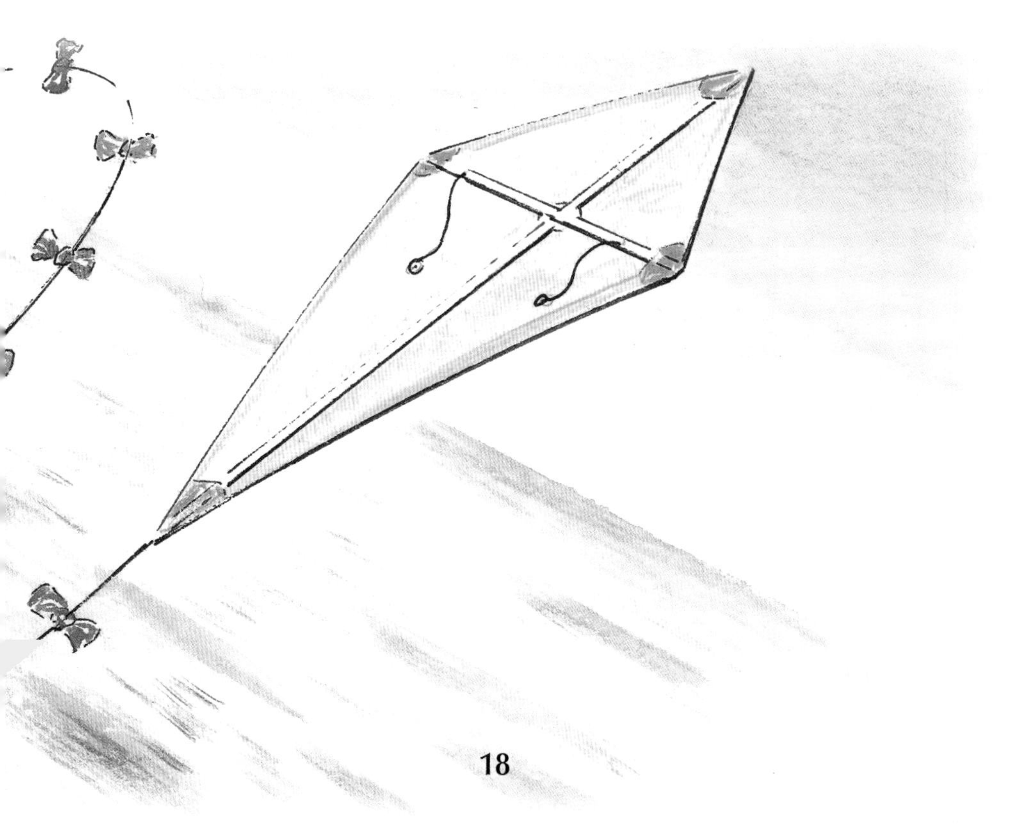

They climbed down off the hedge and walked over to see where the kite had landed.

"Well, that's the end of that." Said Penrose sadly. "I bet it's broken now!"

"Yes, probably." Sighed Pixie.

Then she looked about her and realised that they were no longer in the field where they were told they must play.

Oh dear! Chasing the kite had lead them right to the edge of the cliff!

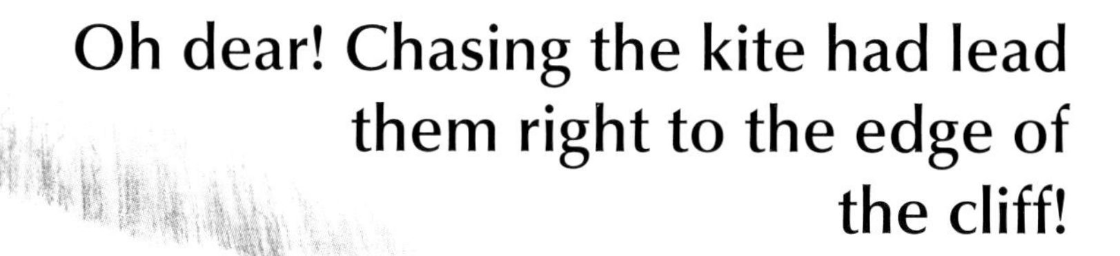

Peter lay down on his tummy and peeked over the cliff edge.

He saw his lovely yellow kite dangling upside down on a bush.

It was broken!

“I can fix it!” Peter said cheerfully looking up at Pixie and Penrose. “It’s only a little tear! If I climb down the cliff a little bit I can reach the tail of bows and pull the kite up!”

“Oh no you will not!” Said Pixie Pasty rather crossly. “We shouldn’t even be here, and as for climbing down the cliff you know how dangerous that can be! What if you get stuck, or worse, fall and hurt yourself! You should know better Peter!”

“I’ll be alright!” Peter said confidently as he clambered over the edge of the cliff and scrambled his way down to the bush.

“Come back Peter! Come back!” Shouted Penrose. But Peter didn’t come back.

Pixie and Penrose lay down on their tummies and watched nervously as Peter stretched out his hand and took hold of the kite tail. He tugged and tugged and soon managed to free the kite from the bush.

“I′ve got it!” He cried happily. “I′m coming back up now!”

Peter tried to scramble his way back up the cliff face, but every time he found a foothold it just crumbled away, and he slipped back down onto the grassy ledge scraping his knees.

"I can't get back up!" He shouted. "I'll have to clamber down to the beach instead!"

Peter tried and tried to find a way down the cliff face to the beach but it was no use, it was far too dangerous! He leaned back against the cliff. It was a long way up and a long way down, what was he going to do? He was stuck!

Tears began to well up in Peters eyes as he realised that he had done a very, very dangerous thing indeed! He was warned not to go near the edge of the cliff and he should never, ever, ever have climbed down!

“Come on Peter! Hurry up!” Shouted Pixie and Penrose.

“I can’t!” Said Peter tearfully. “I can’t climb up and I can’t climb down! I’m stuck! Please help me. I’m really frightened!”

“Oh my goodness!” Said Pixie jumping to her feet. “We have got to get some help Penrose, come on!”

And that is exactly what they did.

Pixie and Penrose ran all the way to Pasty Cottage and raised the alarm.

Daddy Pasty telephoned the emergency services and a rescue helicopter from the Royal Naval Air Station Culdrose took off immediately to try and save Peter from the danger of falling off the cliff.

Peter Patty was absolutely terrified when the helicopter appeared above him.

The noise and the wind from the helicopter blades was tremendous, and he thought he was going to be made deaf before being blown off the face of the cliff.

He cried and cried and wished that he was safe at home.

The Pasty family stood on the cliff
top and watched as one
of the rescue team
was attached to
a winch and
lowered
down to
Peter.

It took
a few
moments
for peter
to be
attached
to the
harness,
because
he was so
frozen with
fear that he
could not move a muscle!

ROYAL NAVY
RESCUE

Eventually the 'thumbs up' signal was given and Peter and his rescuer were winched up to the safety of the helicopter.

It was such an odd sight because Peter Patty still had a hold of his brand new bright yellow kite!

Everyone on the cliff top gave a huge sigh of relief as the pilot gave the helicopter full throttle and sped off in the direction of Treliske Hospital, where Peter was given a thorough check over to make sure that he didn't have any broken bones.

Well, luckily for him he only suffered grazed knees and shock, and both of those have healed quite quickly.

“And that,” said Mummy Pasty, “is why we missed the Culdrose Air Show last year!”

“Goodness Gracious!” Said Grandpop Pasty. “Peter is very, very lucky to have been saved. I do hope he has learned his lesson not to play anywhere near the cliff edge!”

“Oh! He has Grandpop!” Said Penrose. “And he has saved up all his pocket money to give to the Air Sea Rescue Service as a great big thank you for saving his life.”

“My!” Said Grandpop Pasty. “Now that's what I call a very good and kind thing for him to do!”

Grandpop Pasty finished drinking his tea and looked at the clock.

“I am really looking forward to this show.” He said. “When do we leave?”

Toot! Toot! Went the horn of Mr Patty's mini bus.

"Right now!" Said Pixie excitedly. "Let's go Grandpop!"

"Come on everyone." Peter called from the mini bus. "We don't want to miss the show do we?"

"Not this year!" Cried everyone as they trundled down the garden path and climbed aboard the bus.

Peter Patty blushed as he remembered his promise

to

never, ever

climb the dangerous

cliffs again.

And with that they headed off to the spectacular RNAS Culdrose Air Show.

I bet they had a spectacular fun filled day, don't you!

Here are seven words from the story in Cornish. Do you think you can learn them?

Krasa.................................. Toast

Sarf – nyja .... Kite

kordenn .... String

Gwyns .... Wind

Yskynna.......................... Climb

Kleger.............................. Cliff

Peryllus...................Dangerous

WELL DONE!

Cliff Rhyme

I let go of Nanny's hand
And raced her fast across the sand!

Then I said. "Let's climb this cliff!"
"No! No!" Said Nanny with a sniff.

"I know that you are brave and strong,
But, climbing coastal cliffs is wrong!"

Later when I went to bed,
I remembered more that Nanny said.

"A coastal cliff
is not to be,
A climbing frame
for you or me!"

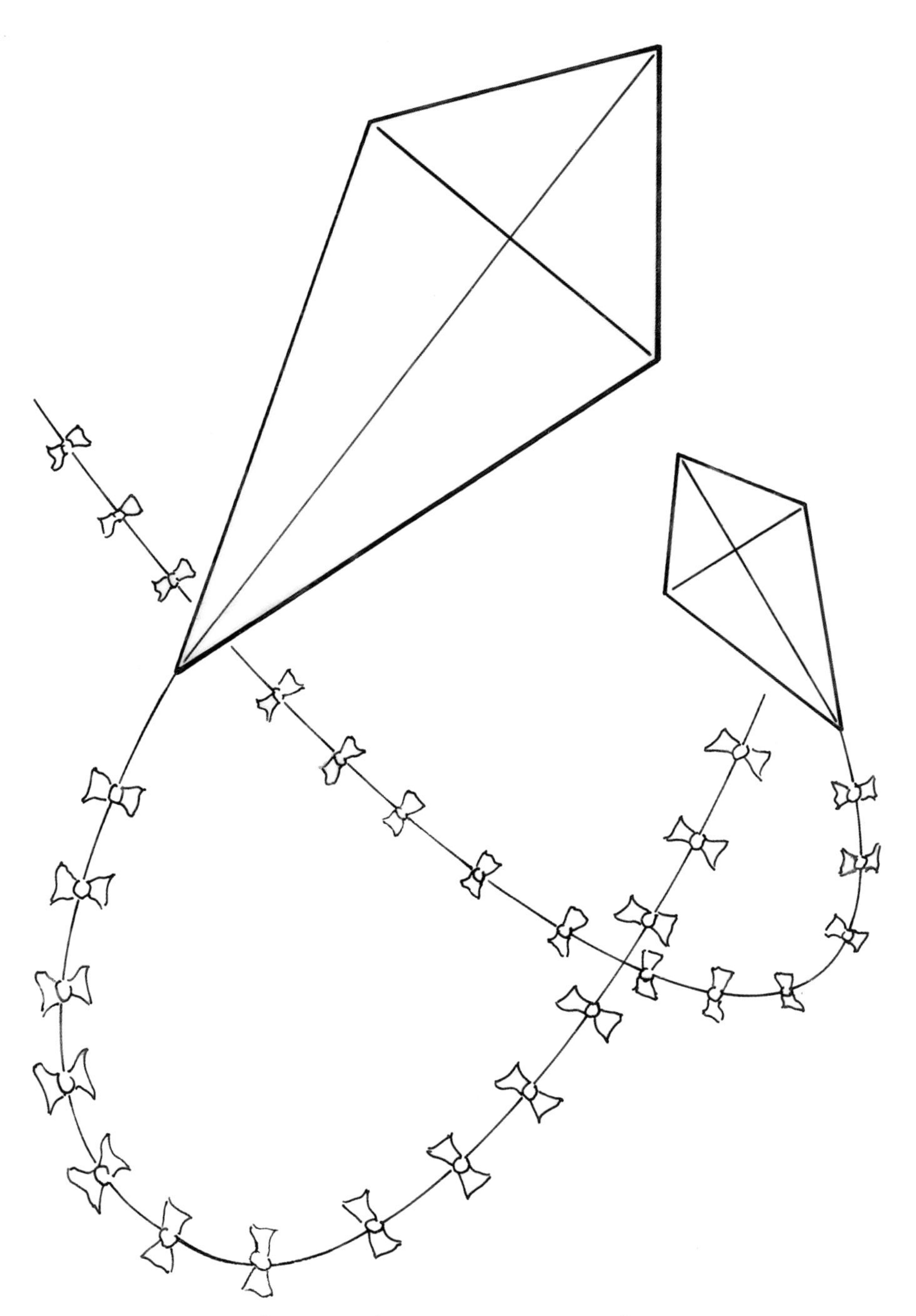

Two kites for you to colour in.

Look for
the next
PASTY PEEPS
adventure.